My Key of Life

我的人生秘诀
（中英双语版）

［美］海伦·凯勒　著

张鲁宁　韩启群　译

中国盲文出版社

图书在版编目（CIP）数据

我的人生秘诀（大字版）/（美）海伦·凯勒（Keller,H.）著；张鲁宁，韩启群译. —北京：中国盲文出版社，2013.1

ISBN 978-7-5002-4050-1

Ⅰ.①我… Ⅱ.①凯… ②张… ③韩… Ⅲ.①散文集—美国—现代 Ⅳ.①I712.65

中国版本图书馆CIP数据核字（2012）第284310号

我的人生秘诀

著　　者：（美）海伦·凯勒
译　　者：张鲁宁　韩启群
策　　划：张　伟
责任编辑：马文莉
出版发行：中国盲文出版社
社　　址：北京市西城区太平街甲6号
邮政编码：100050
印　　刷：北京东君印刷有限公司
经　　销：新华书店
开　　本：787×1092　1/16
字　　数：60千字
印　　张：7.75
版　　次：2013年4月第1版　2013年4月第1次印刷
书　　号：ISBN 978-7-5002-4050-1/I·687
定　　价：15.00元
编辑热线：(010) 83190217
销售服务热线：(010) 83190287　83190288　83190289

版权所有　　侵权必究　　　　　　印装错误可随时退换

我的人生秘诀

My Key of Life

献给我的老师

出 版 说 明

《我的人生秘诀》(My Key of Life)是美国著名盲聋女作家海伦·凯勒在哈佛大学拉德克利夫学院快要毕业时写的一篇长篇哲理散文。文章于1903年首次以《乐观》(Optimism)为名发表,后来重印时采用过书名《我的人生秘诀:乐观》(My Key of Life, Optimism)以及《践行乐观》(The Practice of Optimism)。该文后来也与海伦·凯勒的其他作品合并出版过。

考虑到文章内容以及中英双语形式,此次决定单独出版,并采用书名《我的人生秘诀》(My Key of Life)。

海伦·凯勒创作这篇著名哲理散文距今已一个多世纪,世界社会环境、时代背景已经发生翻天覆地的变化,个别内容在今天读来难以理解。此次出版对类似文字做了适当删节。特此说明。

目 录

出版说明

第一章　内在乐观 ……………………………（1）

我的乐观植根于两个不同的世界，一个是我的内心世界，另一个是我的周围世界。我要求内心世界是美好的，它确实遵循了我的要求；我宣称周围世界是善的，现实中的各种事实也一一印证了我的观点。

第二章　外在乐观 ……………………………（11）

世界上所有伟大的哲学家都是热爱上帝的人，他们对人内心的善深信不疑。了解哲学的历史可以让我们知道，历史上各个时期最伟大的思想家们，无论是部落的预言家还是民族的先知，都是乐观的人。

第三章　践行乐观 ……………………………（31）

乐观是推动社会向前发展的动力，悲观是阻碍世界进步的绊脚石。乐观是一种信念，可以引领人们走向成功。假如心中没有希望，那就注定一事无成。

译　注 ················· （48）

附

My Key of Life ············· （55）

第一章　内在乐观

　　我的乐观植根于两个不同的世界，一个是我的内心世界，另一个是我的周围世界。我要求内心世界是美好的，它确实遵循了我的要求；我宣称周围世界是善的，现实中的各种事实也一一印证了我的观点。

假如我们能够选择所处的环境，假如人类有一种天生的愿望想要成就各种事业，那么，我认为所有的人都是乐观的。毋庸置疑，我们大多数人都认为，获得幸福是所有人奋斗的最终目标。追求幸福的愿望激励着每一个人，包括哲学家、王子，也包括那些清扫烟囱的人。一个人无论多么平庸、碌碌无为，或多么精明强干，都会认为追求幸福是他理所当然的权利。

如果我们留意观察人们对于幸福持有的不同观念，了解他们在什么地方寻找幸福生活的源泉，这是一件很有趣的事情。有些人在积聚财富的过程中寻找幸福，有些人在权力的荣耀里寻找幸福，有些人在艺术和文学的成就中寻找幸福，还有一些人在探索心智或求索知识时寻找幸福。

许多人根据感官的愉悦程度和对物质的占有量来衡量自己有多么幸福。假如他们实现了设定的某一个眼前目标，他们就会感到无比幸福；假如由于缺乏天赋或者条件不允许没有实现，他们则会万分痛苦。如果幸福必须如此衡量的话，那么，像我这样一个看不见也听不到的人就只能坐在角落里掩面哭泣了。

如果我即使看不见也听不到，却仍然感到幸福；如果我的幸福感很强烈，强烈到成为一种信念；如果我的幸福感很深刻，深刻到成为一种生活哲理……简言之，如果我是一个乐观的人，那么这些关于乐观信条的证言就值得一听。既然罪人可以在宗教聚会上起身见证上帝的仁慈，那么饱受磨难的人也可以凭着满怀喜悦的信念站起来见证生活的美好。

曾经，我认为一切都没有希望，四周一片黑暗，后来爱向我走来，释放了我的灵魂；曾经，我只知道黑暗与寂静，现在我知道还有希望与快乐；曾经，我焦躁不安，用身体去撞那堵把我与外界隔开的墙，现在我欣喜地意识到，我能思考并付诸行动，从而到达天国；曾经，我的生活没有过去，也没有将来。悲观的人会说，死亡是"虔诚期待的圆满"。

但是当另外一个人手指间的词语滑落到我的手

上时，尽管无法抓住，我的心却立刻充满了生的渴望。黑夜在思想的白昼到来之前就已逃离，在热切渴求知识的同时，爱、喜悦与希望都来到了我的身边。一个已经摆脱生命囚禁的人，一个已经感受到思想自由带来的激动与狂喜的人，她还会悲观吗？

我早年的经历是从混沌到完美的飞跃。假如我悲观的话，我就不会思考第一次跳出黑暗的原因和动力。勇往直前是我在突然获得解放并奔向光明的那一刻形成的习惯。从可以很灵活地运用第一个单词起，我便学会了生活和思考，并对未来充满了希望。黑暗再也不能把我与外界隔绝。我已经瞥见幸福生活的彼岸，而到达那彼岸的愿望一直在支撑着我的生活。

我的乐观并不是无缘由的微不足道的满足。一位诗人曾经说过，我应该是幸福快乐的，因为我生活在美丽的梦想之中，看不到冰冷残酷的现实。我确实生活在美丽的梦想之中，但那梦想一直是真实的；一点儿也不冰冷，倒是温暖可人；一点儿也不残酷，倒是充满无数祝福。诗人所指的残酷是对现实的一种痛苦觉悟，这个过程是想要充分了解快乐的人所必须经历的。只有接触残酷的现实，才能学会对比地感受真、善、爱的美好。

总是专注于沉思善而忽视恶的存在是错误的，因为灾祸会在人们忽视恶的时候乘虚而入。无知和冷漠状态下的乐观是危险的。不能简单地认为20世纪是人类历史上最好的时代，也不要轻易地在善的美好梦想中寻求逃离恶的世界。有很多好人，事业兴旺发达，生活丰衣足食，他们四下观望时，眼里除了美好别无他物。而此时此刻，他们数以百万计的同伴却像牛羊一样被买卖。当然，也有一些生活舒适的乐观者会认为威尔伯福斯是个爱管闲事的狂热分子，因为他不遗余力地解放黑人奴隶。[1]

对于在这个国家出现的盲目乐观，我深表怀疑，因为在有很多冤屈不平急需纠正之时，这些盲目乐观者却叫嚣着："太好了！一切都没有问题！我们是世界上最伟大的民族。"这显然是错误的乐观。没有付出任何代价的乐观就如同建在沙滩上的房子。要把自己描述为一个乐观的人，并期待别人相信自己完全可以拥有那样的信仰，就必须理解什么是苦难，就必须经历悲痛。

我知道苦难是什么，也曾经与它有过一两次交手，有一段时间还曾深切感受到它在我生活中的可怕影响。因此，我很有底气地说，苦难没什么大不了的，只不过是精神训练操而已。正是由于我曾经接触过苦难，所以我变得更加乐观。我可以很肯定地说，和苦难的斗争是上帝最好的祝福，它使我们更加坚忍不拔，成为社会的栋梁之才。它引领我们触摸到万物的灵魂，使我们明白，这个世界虽然充满苦难，但同时还有很多战胜这些苦难的办法。

我的乐观并不在于我没有遇到不幸，而是在于我乐于相信这个世界上绝大部分地方都有善，愿意努力地和善合作，并相信它最终会取得胜利。我努力增强上帝赋予我的力量，尝试看待每个人、每件物的最好之处，并让它成为我生活的一部分。这个世界上到处都播下了善的种子，但是，只有将自己积极的思想付诸实施，并坚持在自己的土地上辛勤耕耘，才能收获善的精华。

我的乐观植根于两个不同的世界，一个是我的内心世界，另一个是我的周围世界。我要求内心世界是美好的，它确实遵循了我的要求；我宣称周围世界是善的，现实中的各种事实也一一印证了我的观点。我向美好敞开胸襟，把丑恶拒之门外。这就是执著拥有美好信念的力量，它存在于任何事物的对立面。我从来没有因为看不到美好而心生气馁，也绝不会因与人争辩而失去希望。怀疑和不信任只是思想胆怯而导致的恐慌，坚强的意志可以将它击得粉碎，而宽广的心胸则可以战胜一切。

大学时光即将结束，我感到无比激动，怀揣着美好的梦想期待未来。在这个世界上我只能承担有限的工作，但正是这样才使工作显得弥足珍贵，而且渴望工作的意愿也是心态乐观的体现。

大约六十年前，卡莱尔[2]忘我地投入到传播福音的工作中。而那些幻想家则徜徉于幸福的空中楼阁，对法国大革命怀有无限的憧憬，而一旦必定要来的狂风将楼阁刮倒时，他们就变得悲观了。面对这些丧失行动能力的恩底弥翁、阿拉斯托尔、维特[3]们，这位身处艰难现实世界仍怀有梦想的苏格兰农民喊出了自己的劳动信条："别再混沌了，回到有秩序的世界来吧。生产！生产！哪怕是生产出一个产品的最微不足道的部件，以上帝的名义！这是你可以竭尽所能之处，不要忘记这一点，努力，努力！无论手边有什么可以做的事情，尽最大努力做好。在白天工作吧，因为当黑夜来临，无论何地都没有人能够工作。"

有人曾这样评论，卡莱尔吩咐别人面朝黄土背朝天地辛苦劳作，自己却从辛劳中逃脱，因此他不知道他人的艰辛。但卡莱尔并不是这样想的。"愚蠢！"他说道，"理想就在你头脑里，障碍也在你内心里。从贫穷苦难的现实中找到理想，积极生活，认真思索，坚定信念，最终获得自由！"多么朴实无华的言辞！正是工作和生产帮助人们从混沌中发现生机，让个体回归有秩序的世界，而这种秩序正是乐观的体现。

同样，我也可以工作，因为我热爱用自己的双手和大脑劳动。无论怎样我都是一个乐观的人。以前，我常常认为我想做点儿有用之事的愿望肯定会遭遇挫折。但是后来我发现，虽然我能够发挥作用的方式寥寥无几，但在我面前却有做不完的工作。

葡萄园里最快乐的采摘工人可能是个腿有残疾的人，虽然其他采摘工人可以很容易地超越他的工作量。每当葡萄园的葡萄在阳光下成熟时，他会开心地掂量着一串串饱满的葡萄。

达尔文一次只能工作半小时，但就在这些勤勤恳恳的半小时里，他却为哲学奠定了新的基础。

我一直想要完成一件伟大而高尚的事情，但是，完成那些微不足道的工作是我主要的责任和快乐，仿佛它们就是伟大而高尚的事情。我需要思考如何更好地完成每天要完成的工作，并为有些事我不能做但别人能做而感到高兴。

历史学家格林[4]告诉我们，世界的运转并不仅仅只靠英雄们的大力推动，也依赖于每位诚实劳动者微薄助推的合力。这种思想足以为在这个黑暗世界里的我指明方向。我热爱他人付出的善，因为他们的付出确保了一点，即无论我是否有用，真和善都会永远存在下去。

我相信自己，没有任何事情可以动摇我乐观的信念。我认识到了所有人膜拜的至高力量——秩序、命运、圣灵、自然、上帝——带来的益处。我认识到太阳哺育万物、延续生命的力量。我与这些不可名状的力量结为朋友，立刻感到全身充满力量，勇敢地迎接上天为我安排的任何命运。这便是我对乐观的信仰！

第二章　外在乐观

世界上所有伟大的哲学家都是热爱上帝的人，他们对人内心的善深信不疑。了解哲学的历史可以让我们知道，历史上各个时期最伟大的思想家们，无论是部落的预言家还是民族的先知，都是乐观的人。

乐观其实一直存在于我内心深处。不过，在审视自己周围的外在世界时，我的内心也没有矛盾。外部世界验证了我的内心对善的信奉。纵观我在大学读书的那些年，阅读一直在帮助我不断地发现善的存在。在文学、哲学、宗教和历史典籍里，我找到了有关我信仰的有力见证。

哲学就是一部盲聋人的历史。从苏格拉底的谈话到柏拉图、贝克莱和康德，哲学记录了人类智慧为冲破物质世界的藩篱进入纯粹思想世界所付出的种种努力。

一个盲聋人应该能从柏拉图的"理想国"中寻找到特别的意义。我们的所见、所闻、所感往往并不是现实的真实面目，只是思想、原则、精神的并不完美的体现；思想、原则、精神揭示真理，而我们的所见、所闻、所感都是错觉。

假如真的如此，我的明眼同胞兄弟姐妹们在充分享受五官带来的愉悦时，并没有意识到你们看到的现实世界和我心目中所感触到的世界未必一样。哲学赋予心灵发现真理的特权，引领我们进入一个领域，这是一个眼睛看不见的我与健全的你们没有任何区别的王国。

贝克莱认为人的双眼看到的其实是事物颠倒的图像，然后大脑无意识地将图像纠正过来。当我了解到这一点时，我开始怀疑眼睛，认为它们并不是很可靠的工具；同时心里很高兴，仿佛恢复了和别人一样的平等权利。但我感到高兴，不是因为感官用处很小，而是因为心智与精神在上帝永恒的世界里大有作为。

对我而言，哲学似乎就是用来特别安慰我的，由此我算是和某些现代哲学家扯平了，他们认为我希望成为他们那些特定教导的试验者。但是，我的个人经历也在特定范围内用弱小的声音表达一个哲学宣言：善是唯一的世界，世界是精神的世界。同时，它也是个秩序统治一切的世界，不变的逻辑将所有分散的部分联系在一起，一切井然有序，不存在混乱。在这个世界里，恶如圣奥古斯丁所言，只是幻觉，因此是不存在的。

哲学对于我的意义并不仅仅在于理论，更重要的是在于一个事实，即提出理论的伟大哲学家们与外部世界快乐地隔绝，极少与外界接触，甚至就像柏拉图和莱布尼茨一样只是在庭院和休息室走动。他们听不到生活的喧嚣，看不到令人眼花缭乱、心烦意乱的生活百态。他们独自静坐，但不是在黑暗里，试图从自己的内心发现一切。即使从自己的内心一无所获，他们仍然坚信，只要能够远离尘嚣，思考上帝的智慧，他们就能找到真理。这些伟大的神秘主义者一人独处，听不到、看不见任何东西，只是与上帝为伴。

　　荷兰哲学家斯宾诺莎[1]曾被逐出教会，穷困潦倒，而且还遭到犹太教和基督教的蔑视与猜疑，但是我能够理解，当时他为什么还能够寻找到内心深处源源不断的快乐与幸福。这并不是因为我遭遇了和他类似的情形，而是因为他远离感官愉悦的世界，与我的经历多少有些相似。他热爱善是出于善本身的原因。与很多伟大的灵魂一样，他接受自己在世界中的位置，像孩子一样将自己托付给更高的神灵，认为神灵会占据他的内心，通过他的双手成就工作。他对此深信不疑，而那也是我所深信的。

在我看来，强烈而又神圣的乐观应该源自这样一种坚定的信仰，即上帝会在我们每个个体的身上体现出来。这个上帝不是遥远的、难以企及的宇宙主宰，而是一个离我们每个人都很近的上帝。他不仅会出现在大地、海洋和天空，更重要的是，他会出现在我们心脏每一次纯洁、神圣的跳动时，他是"所有心灵的源泉与中心，是它们唯一的归宿"。

我从哲学中了解到，我们看到的只是影子，知道的只是片面的知识，万事万物都是变化的。但是，心智，正是不可战胜的心智包括了所有真理，接受宇宙，将影子转变为现实，使尘世中喧嚣的变化成为永恒沉寂中点点滴滴的片断，或者是不断追求至善的条条捷径，使罪恶成为通向"至善之路的短暂停留"。

我通过双手只能抓住世界的一个微小部分，但是我的心灵却可以使我看到整个世界，我的思想可以使我理解操控世界的仁慈法则。这些观念激发的信心与信任教会我安然面对生活，接受上帝的安排，不再疑神疑鬼，免受了各种恐惧的困扰。确实，我得到了上帝的庇佑，虽然看不见，但心里却深信不疑。

世界上所有伟大的哲学家都是热爱上帝的人，他们对人内心的善深信不疑。了解哲学的历史可以让我们知道，历史上各个时期最伟大的思想家们，无论是部落的预言家还是民族的先知，都是乐观的人。

哲学的发展史就是人类精神生活的故事典籍。展现在我们面前的大量的各种事件，我们称之为历史。在观看这些事件时，我发现它们是按照上帝的方式发展形成的。人类的历史也是一部伟大的进步史诗。无论在内部世界还是外部世界，我都看到了奇妙的和谐统一，看到了无与伦比的象征，它揭示了人与圣灵之间的亲密交流，也彰显了在现实中不断重复的哲理。人类历史的各个组成部分里都隐藏了善的精神，而这种精神也使整个人类历史有了意义。

追溯至人类历史之初时，我看到原始人类试图从大自然的巨大威力中逃脱。此时，他们还不知道如何驾驭自然，只是寻求让超自然的神灵息怒，正是这些超自然的存在导致了他们对神灵的恐惧。随着思想的进步，我看到原始人类解放了，变得文明了，不再敬畏那些面目狰狞的不可知的神灵。经历了无数艰难困苦，他们终于学会在头顶上空建立屋顶，使起居不受自然的影响，也使家园免遭破坏。他们在自己的国土上兴建庙宇，敬奉充满喜悦的光神和歌神。他们从艰难困苦中懂得了公平和正义，在与同伴的争斗中学会了辨明是非，这使他们成为了有思想、有道德的人。他们被赋予了希腊天才式的秉性与智慧。

不过希腊也不是完美无瑕的。她的那些理想化的目标和宗教观念距离具体实践十分遥远，因此她消逝在历史的长河中，但是她的那些理想会留存下来，以励后世。

同样，罗马也为世界留下了丰富的遗产。在历史的变迁中，她的法则和有序的管理已经成为不同时期辉煌的实体典范。但是，当她坚强朴实的人民不再是她文明的力量和支柱时，罗马陨落了。

接着，北方诸多新国家诞生了，更加永久的新社会建立了。希腊和罗马社会的基础是奴隶，他们受尽剥削压迫，过着悲惨不幸的生活。他们"在田野劳动，在作坊工作，精疲力竭，就像套上缰绳的马匹，如果把眼睛蒙上的话，会一声不响"。新社会的基础是自由人，他们不断斗争，辛勤耕作，善于判断，人数也越来越多。他们把部族的亲属关系改制为州邦，培育出任何压迫都不能摧垮的独立与自强的精神。人类从带有兽性的原始社会开始，经历了野蛮愚昧和不断自我征服的过程，最终发展到文明社会。这种漫长的发展史就是乐观主义精神的体现。从新社会诞生的那一刻起，欧洲在每个世纪都有长足的发展，这种状况一直持续到美国应世界发展的需要出现为止。

托尔斯泰说过，美国曾经一度是世界的希望，但是却遭到贪欲之神的束缚。要想了解美国人民正在进行的独一无二的公民斗争，托尔斯泰与其他欧洲人还需要了解许多有关我们自由而伟大祖国的知识。她正面临一项巨大工程，那就是要吸收并同化从不同国家聚集到美国来的所有外国人，并将他们打造成拥有统一民族精神的一个大民族。在美利坚合众国展示她能否将来自世界各国的移民重新塑造成一个新的民族之前，我们有权要求批评者保持忍耐。

伦敦的六百万人口中约有五十万为非本土出生，对此伦敦的经济学家们感到恐慌，开始煞有介事地讨论太多外族人口带来的危险。但是，在纽约，三百五十万人口中有一百五十万人为非本土出生，与此相比，伦敦的问题又算什么呢？想一想，我们美国的大都市里每三个人中就有一个是非本土出生的！单从这些数字中就可以看出美国的伟大！

的确，美国付出了很多精力来解决物质上的问题——开垦荒田，开采矿山，浇灌沙漠，修建横贯东西的铁路。但是，在做这些事情时，她采用了一种全新的方式，即教育民众，根据每个人的不同需求安排其学习技能和才干。她把工业获得的财富投入到对劳动人民的教育事业之中。这样一来，没有一技之长的人在美国就会难以立足，每个人都要通过自己的聪明才智来获得财富。她的子民不是苦工，也不是奴隶。对此，美国宪法已经作了明确的宣布，我们国家体制的精神也加强了这一点。他们应该明白这片土地能够教给他们最好的东西。他们将会知道，在这个国家没有上层阶级，也没有下层阶级；他们将会理解，上帝和他的国为每个人准备的是怎样一幅光景。

即使美国做到了这一切，她可能仍然是自私的，是玛门[2]的崇拜者。不过，美国既是商业的热土，也是慈善的源头。走在车水马龙的大街上，站在喧嚣的工厂旁边，望着高耸入云的百货大楼，你可以看到学校、图书馆、医院、公园，这些都是展现大众仁爱之心的作品，是融入了不朽思想的财富象征。为了减少人们的痛苦，让所有饱经苦难的人重新融入社会，美国已经付出了很多努力，如帮助盲人用手指感受视觉，教聋哑人说话，让智障之人恢复心智等。

看着这一切，请告诉我她是不是真的只崇尚物质财富？她以博大的同情与怜爱，娴熟的技能和聪明才智帮助所有投奔她的人。每年全世界有很多国家向美国求助，她总是努力减轻这些国家日益严峻的贫困，减少他们不断增加的不幸，减缓他们日渐严重的衰退进程。对此，谁来加以衡量呢？

在我思索这些事实的时候，不禁想到，与托尔斯泰以及其他一些理论家相反，我觉得身为美国人是一件很光荣的事情。在美国，乐观之人有数不尽的理由对现实充满信心，对未来抱有希望。而这种信心与希望也会传播到世界上所有伟大的国度。

假如把我们所处的时代与过去进行比较，便会在现代统计学里发现乐观主义在全世界有着坚实的基础，这种乐观轻松活泼、充满自信。虽然在我们的周围充斥着彷徨、不安和对物质的崇拜，但是，在这背后，一种坚定的信念正在世上最美好的生活里闪闪发光。假如听信悲观之人，就会认为文明在中世纪就已安营扎寨，从此再没有收到前进的命令。但是，他并没有意识到历史进步的车轮并非从不中断前进。

"人类总体是在进步，但是也有往复。生活艰辛，前进之路充满变数。"

这是我最近刚读到的一篇演讲，作者知识渊博，无人可以望其项背。[3]他的演讲中有大量关于人类进步的实证。

过去的五十年间，犯罪率一直在下降。应当承认，当前的犯罪记录名单比过去更长，但是我们的统计也比过去更为全面、准确，而且记录名单上的罪行有很多在半个世纪以前并没有被视为是犯罪。这一点说明公众的良知和道德观念变得比以往更为进步。

我们对犯罪的定义已经越来越严格，对犯罪的惩罚也越来越仁慈、巧妙。以前存在的复仇情绪基本上消失了，不再是以牙还牙，以眼还眼。罪犯被当成是心智不健全的人。他们被判入狱不仅仅出于惩罚，而且因为他们对社会构成了威胁。在服刑期间，他们受到了人性的关爱，也受到纪律的约束。这样一来，他们心智的疾病就会被治愈，然后重新回到社会，承担起应该承担的工作与责任。

公众良知的觉醒和萌发的另一个标志是努力为工人阶级提供更好的居住条件。一百年前会有人去思考贫苦大众的住处也应该干净方便、阳光明媚吗？不要忘记在"美好的往日"（"Good Old Times"）霍乱和伤寒病曾经毁掉整座县城，瘟疫远走异乡，在欧洲国家的首都肆虐。

如今，不光是劳动人民住进了条件较好的房子，有了环境更好的工作场所，而且雇主也意识到被雇用的工人有权利追求更高的工资待遇。从现代工业斗争的黑暗和混乱中，我们能够隐隐约约地洞悉隐藏在这些斗争背后的一些道理。应当承认每个人都有生的权利，同时还有获得自由和追求幸福的权利，并像伯克[4]所梦想的那样，具有主动安抚他人的精神，强势群体愿意向弱势群体作出让步，认识到雇主的权利其实是与雇用工人的权利捆绑在一起的——正是从这些变化中，乐观的人看到了我们这个时代的特征。

受教育的权利是美国已承认的属于每个公民的另一个权利。在欧洲和美国的开明地区，每座城市、每个乡镇、每个村庄都有自己的学校。学校不再只是某个阶级获取知识的地方，学校的大门也同样向最穷苦的劳动者的儿女敞开。自文明国家诞生起，全民教育就在扫除目不识丁的文盲。

教育面不断拓宽，包括了所有人；教育内容愈加深入，触及了所有真理。学者们不再仅仅局限于研究希腊语、拉丁语和数学，他们也在研究科学。科学可以使诗人的梦想成真，让数学家的猜想、经济学家的理论变为舰船、医院和各种仪器，进而使一个技术娴熟的工人能够完成从前需要一千个工人才能完成的工作。如今的学生不会被问及有没有学习语法。他是不是只是一架语法机器，或是一沓有关科学发现的干瘪目录？他是不是拥有男子气概的必备品质？对他来说，最重要的课程应该是学会设法解决公众关心的重要问题，愿意接受新思想和关于真理的新观点，重拾在追逐财富过程中失去的美好理想，努力促进人与人之间的公平与正义。他知道人的繁重劳动或许有其他东西可以替代，比如马力、机器或者书本知识，但是"常识、耐心、诚实与勇气却没有任何东西可以替代"。

如果看到盲人和聋哑人现在的状况与一个世纪

以前相比的巨大差异，谁还能怀疑教育的伟大功绩和显著成就呢？一个世纪以前，盲人和聋哑人被认为是一群遭了诅咒的人，命运与社会最底层的乞丐相似。每个人都认为他们的生活毫无希望可言，这种境况使他们陷入深深的绝望之中。

阿维[5]主动提出教盲人读书，而盲人自己竟然感觉很可笑。他们所处的环境只能使他们对生活没有任何美好的愿望，对于任何想要拯救他们脱离苦难的举动，他们都会认为是精神错乱之人的异常表现。这种残酷环境给他们带来的不可名状的禁闭感是多么令人感到遗憾啊！但是现在，看看这些变化和革新吧！专门为盲人成立的组织机构和工业公司就像魔术表演一般神奇地大量出现；很多聋哑人不仅学会了读书写字，还学会了说话。请记住：豪博士[6]的信念与耐心已经开花结果，他在各地积极开展盲人和聋哑人教育，鼓励他们与现实生活抗争。现在的我也是充满希望，信心百倍。对此，你是不是感到惊讶呢？

教育的最高成就便是学会包容。长久以来，人类为了自身的信仰而战,并为之献身。但是,培养人们具有另外一种勇气却花了很长时间,即要求人们认可其他同胞的信仰,承认这些同胞也有维护自己道德标准的权利。包容是社会的第一准则,是一种精神,保持着人类认为最珍贵的东西。洪水与闪电给人类带来了巨大损失,大自然的敌对力量破坏了很多城市和庙宇。虽然这些灾难夺取了许多人的宝贵生命,几乎使人类丧失前进的动力,但是这一切都远远比不上由于人类自身缺乏包容带来的伤害。

带着一丝惊讶与伤感,我追忆起人类不能相互包容且非常偏执的年代。我仿佛看到主耶稣遭到嘲笑和蔑视,被钉在十字架上;主耶稣的追随者遭到追捕,受尽折磨,甚至被活活烧死。我想到那些拒绝接受中世纪迷信的杰出人物,他们被指责为对上帝不敬而惨遭杀害。我仿佛又看到以色列的子民受尽辱骂,被那些口头上伪称是基督徒的人迫害致死;他们从一个国家被驱赶到另一个国家,从一个避难所被追杀到另一个避难所,被传唤到关押重罪犯人的地方,遭到严刑拷打。他们强忍着殉难的痛苦，仍然宣称他们自始至终都抱有的信仰，却遭到无情的嘲笑。这双曾迫害犹太人的偏执魔爪同样也伸向了基督教中不信奉国教的人，凶残地对付这些纯洁无辜的生命，铲除消灭了阿尔比派[7]以及和平安宁的韦尔多派[8]，使他们"尸横遍野，凄惨无比"。

我慢慢回想着人类历史上的这些污点，耳边似乎想起了竭力反对偏执的呼号。摆脱偏执的宽容之手被置于审判官面前，人文主义者向那些受到迫害的人传达了和平的信息。再不会有"烧死异教徒"的高声呐喊，人们开始以怜悯之心思索人类的灵魂，心中油然而生的是一股对看不见的上帝的新的敬畏。

珍惜手足情谊的观点再次出现在这个世界，其内涵更加广阔，不仅仅局限于某个教派或支持某个教义的成员之间的有限团结。像莱辛[9]这样有着伟大心灵的思想家向这个世界提出了质疑：到底是宗教间的仇恨和鱼死网破般的激烈冲突能彰显上帝的荣耀，还是齐心协力、互相帮助更能体现上帝的作为呢？

如今，人与人之间古已有之的偏见在宽厚仁慈的情感光辉的照耀之下开始消融退却，这种情感不会为了外在的形式而牺牲他人的生命，也不会剥夺人们从各自的信仰中所获得的慰藉和力量。一个时代的异端邪说到了下一个时代往往就成了正统学说。只有包容才能赋予各个宗教派别的虔诚信徒们兄弟姐妹般的情感。乐观的人为天主教徒和新教教徒内心深处的团结友爱、情意相投而感到高兴。关于这种情感，我们可以从全世界所有善良之人对教皇利奥十三世[10]的顶礼膜拜与热情赞美中找到示范。所有教派的信徒都向纯洁的灵魂致敬，祭奠他们，为爱默生[11]和钱宁[12]举行的百年诞辰纪念就是最好的例证。

凭借我对当前所处时代的理解，我发现我非常乐意做这个世界的公民。就我所处的国家而言，我觉得做一名美国人就意味着是一个乐观的人。我知道我们国家在菲律宾土地上做了一些毫不公平的事情，令人很不愉快。但我相信这是治国策略的失误，这个民族真正的智慧并没有完全发挥出来。

恺撒大帝的历史告诉我们，在无休止的内战中，有数以百万计爱好和平的牧民和其他劳动人民，只要条件允许就会投入工作。他们会在少数人率领的大军到来之前撤离，然后就在某处等待，待到危险一过，他们就会返回家园，耐心地修缮战争中遭到破坏的一切。这些人民有耐心，秉性诚实，然而他们的统治者却走入歧途。

我很欣喜地看到，在这个世界，在我们的国家，出现了一种崭新的、更好的爱国主义精神，比原来那种要置敌人于死地的爱国精神更好！这种爱国主义精神比战场上的更加崇高。它引领数以千万计的人们为服务社会而愿意献出一切，乃至生命，每一个躺下的生命都会把我们向着农田不再变为战场的和平时代推进一步。所以，尽管听说菲律宾战场上的战斗异常残酷，我并没有感到绝望，因为我心里知道，广大人民的心并不在那场战斗上，破坏和平的人必须适时停止。

第三章 践行乐观

乐观是推动社会向前发展的动力,悲观是阻碍世界进步的绊脚石。乐观是一种信念,可以引领人们走向成功。假如心中没有希望,那就注定一事无成。

检验各种信仰的办法是衡量它在生活中的实际作用。乐观是推动社会向前发展的动力，悲观是阻碍世界进步的绊脚石。假设这种观点是正确的，那么传播悲观主义哲学就是非常有害的行为。如果一个人认为世界上的痛苦超过快乐，并且表达出这种抑郁的观点，那么他的痛苦就只会有增无减。

由此看来，叔本华[1]的哲学观确实是人类的敌人。即使他确实认为大千世界充满了苦难和不幸，也不应该将这种信念广为宣传，因为这会削弱人们与逆境抗争的斗志。如果生活让他吃了炉灰，而不是面包，他也不应该怨天尤人。[2]人生是一个公平的战场，只要我们时刻准备奋斗，正义的事业就能成功。

一旦悲观主义占据了人的心灵，生活就会变得乱七八糟，精神也会因此充满苦恼和空虚。没有什么特效药能够治愈这种个人生活的无序或社会秩序的混乱，只有忘记这一切或者将之彻底毁灭。

悲观的人会说："我们吃吧，喝吧，尽情享乐吧，因为明天我们就会死去。"假如以他们的眼光审视我的生活，我应该算是彻底无望了。我努力寻找从来没有出现在我眼里的光明，寻找从来没有在我耳边响起的音乐，结果应该是徒劳无获；我日日夜夜地祈求，应该是从未得到任何应许；我一个人孤独无助地独处，内心应该完全被恐惧和绝望所占据。然而，我成功摆脱了所有的痛苦和不幸，即使这种不幸比其他任何生理缺陷所导致的不幸都要严重。因为在我看来，活得快乐幸福不仅是对自己负责，也是对别人负责。

一个看不到希望或体会不到美好的人怎么能让自己的观点影响他人，使他人丧失勇气呢？而那些人可能正背负着上帝特别赐予的重担。

乐观的人绝不能犹豫，绝不能退缩，因为他知道，如果自己掉队的话，就会阻碍后面的人前进。因此，他要无畏无惧地坚守在队伍中，牢记不说泄气的话。每个人的内心都承受了足够多的痛苦与不幸。他要用自己的双手拿起逆境的铁钩，把它们当做工具，清除挡在前进道路上的每一个障碍。他会继续努力奋斗，就好像独自肩负着在人间重建天堂的重任。

我们知道，世界上的哲学家都是乐观的人，他们是理论家；所有付诸行动的人和建功立业的人也是乐观的人，他们是实干家。

豪博士找到了触及劳拉·布里奇曼[3]心灵的方法，因为他从一开始就相信自己可以做到。英国法理学家曾说过，从法律角度来看，聋哑人和盲人是心智不健全的人。看看乐观的人是怎么做的吧！豪博士竭力反驳这条冰冷无情的法律公理。在聋哑人和盲人迟钝、麻木而冷漠的肉体之下，他看到了其被束缚的心灵，而后他平静果断地解救了这被缚的灵魂。他的努力最终获得了成功，近似白痴的人被赋予了常人的智慧。同时，他也向法律证明，聋哑人和盲人同样也是具有责任感的人。

阿维主动请缨教授盲人读书时，一群悲观的人嘲笑他愚蠢又荒唐。假如他没有坚信人类的心灵远远比束缚它的无知更有力量，假如他不是一个乐观的人，他就不可能把盲人的手指变为认识世界的新工具。

从来没有哪个悲观的人能发现新星的秘密，也从来没有哪个悲观的人能够成功驶向地图上某个未描绘的地域，或开拓出人类精神世界的极乐之地。

圣伯纳德教士[4]是一个非常坚定的乐观主义者，他相信二百五十个得到启迪的人可以驱散笼罩十字军东征时期的黑暗。他个人信仰所发出的光芒，点亮了西欧历史的一个新篇章。

圣约翰·鲍思高[5]也是一个乐观的人，在意大利各个城市里，他是那些穷人和无依无靠者的恩人。作为一个先知，他感悟到了看似遥远的神的旨意，不遗余力地向同胞们传递来自天国的消息。虽然人们对他的种种预言嗤之以鼻，称他为疯子，可他还是继续耐心地工作，用自己的双手为流浪街头的儿童提供庇护。鲍思高满怀热忱地预测，一定会有一个伟大运动发端于他所做的工作。在尚未获得资金和赞助的时候，他就描绘了一幅幅有着辉煌体系的蓝图，这个体系里布满了很多学校和医院，它们会出现在意大利的每一个角落。他在有生之年看到了圣萨尔瓦多会的建立，这正是他敢于积极预言的乐观主义的体现。

塞甘博士[6]在宣布智障者可以接受教育时也同样遭到了人们的嘲笑，这些人自命不凡地说塞甘本人比白痴强不了多少。但是塞甘这个高尚而又乐观的人坚持了下来。不久之后，那些顽固不化的悲观者发现，曾经遭到他们嘲笑戏弄的人已经成了世界著名的慈善家。

乐观的人坚持信念，敢于尝试，最后能够成就大事。乐观的人总是心情愉快，沐浴在灿烂的阳光里。等到有一天，那美妙而难以言说的上帝的国降临时，上帝的荣光照耀着他，而他就在那里迎接它的到来。他常常与自己的灵魂相遇，时时吹奏着欢快的进行曲向另一个新的发现前进，争取一次又一次地战胜艰难险阻，从而不断地增加知识，获得幸福。

我们已经发现，伟大的哲学家和实干家都是乐观向上的人。那些最具号召力的作家无论在他们的作品里还是在现实生活中都是乐观的人。而悲观的作家无论多么才华出众，都不可能赢得大量的读者。许多乐观的作家读者众多，被人们广为敬仰，甚至超越了他们自身的才华，正是因为他们描绘了生活中阳光的一面。

狄更斯、兰姆、哥德史密斯、欧文等作家深受读者的爱戴，他们儒雅风趣，都是积极乐观的人。而一向悲观的斯威夫特[7]虽然才华出众，无人能及，却从来没有拥有过与其才华相匹配的读者数量。的确，18世纪的斯威夫特如果在我们这个时代遇到了萨克雷[8]，很难受到这位慷慨乐观的人的公平对待。

尽管奥马尔·海亚姆的《鲁拜集》[9]在后世没有获得很好的声名，但我们仍可以得出这样一条准则：任何对社会有影响的作家都必须是个有信仰的人，必须以乐观主义作为自己最基本的人生准则。当然，他也可以像卡莱尔和罗斯金那样，时而怒吼，时而争执，时而又感到悔恨，但是他所有的工作都必须基于一个最根本的信条，即相信人生以及整个世界一定会变得更美好。

在乐观向上的人中，莎士比亚称得上是佼佼者。他的悲剧作品揭示了社会的道德秩序。在戏剧

《李尔王》和《哈姆雷特》中,他不但表达了对美好事物的向往,而且还在这两部戏的结尾处安排了一个角色去匡扶正义,恢复社会秩序,重新建立国家。他晚期创作的戏剧《暴风雨》和《辛白林》展示了美妙而又平静的乐观,表现了一种为和解和团聚而感到由衷喜悦的乐观,目的是为了实现外部世界的善和内心深处的善的最终胜利。

假如勃朗宁[10]的作品没有那么晦涩,那他肯定是统治本世纪诗坛的诗人了。当他高呼"啊,看这金秋的清晨,古老的大地绽放灿烂的美好笑容"时,我感到一种心醉神迷的快乐。"正因为世上有不完美,所以才肯定有完美;完整肯定来自残缺;失败也是一种胜利,因为它使生活充实。"这些诗句使我思绪万千。的确,不和谐是存在的,或许和谐就是来自不和谐;病痛破坏了健康,而健康可以恢复;我看不见也听不见,或许其他遭受同样痛苦折磨的人能比我看得更清楚,比我听得更明白。勃朗宁告诉我们,不存在失去的善,这个道理让我可以更轻松地面对生活。不管对错,不要害怕,只要尽自己最大的努力。我的内心在自豪地回应他的劝导：乐于偿还生活让你背负的各种债务，包括痛苦、黑暗和冷漠；勇于接受生活的挑战，承担责任，这是上帝赐予的礼物！

假如作家的思想要广为传播，他必须是一个乐观向上的人，因为他的思想大多是对其生活经历的总结。斯蒂文森[11]死后仅十年，他的生活方式就成为了典范。他在众多文人墨客中占据一席之地，是自约翰逊[12]和兰姆[13]之后最有气魄的作家。记得有一段时间，由于一直努力在做的工作总是完成不了，我感到心灰意冷，几近放弃。正当我感到困惑沮丧时，我读到斯蒂文森的一篇随笔。顿时，我感觉就像是伴着阳光外出郊游了一番，不再为困难的工作感到垂头丧气。我重新鼓起勇气，再次投入到工作之中，甚至在我自己还没有意识到的情况下，工作就顺利地完成了。后来，我也失败过很多次，但自从意志坚定的布道者斯蒂文森教我要以"微笑的方式"去面对挫折之后，我再也没有像以前那样感到沮丧和气馁。

读叔本华和奥马尔的著作，就会慢慢发现我们的世界虚无缥缈，正如他们描述的那样。

读格林所著的英格兰历史，就会发现我们的世界到处都是英雄。我读了格林的传记之后，才明白为什么格林笔下的历史让我兴奋不已，让我感受到浪漫传奇故事的神奇力量。再后来，我知道了他如何用丰富的想象力把枯燥单调的历史史实变为了新鲜生动的梦想。在格林和妻子穷得连炉火都生不起的日子里，他会坐在没有生火的壁炉边，想象着炉火正在熊熊燃烧。他说道："要不断提炼思想，把沮丧挡在门外，向着光明呐喊。闭上眼睛沉思默想得到的智慧远远比那些迂腐的哲学家能给予你的要多得多。"

乐观的人总是与进步同行，并且会促进进步的步伐，而悲观的人却会使世界停滞不前。悲观对国家发展的影响与对个人生命历程的影响是一样的。悲观会扼杀激励人们与贫穷、无知及罪恶作斗争的天性，耗尽世上所有的喜悦之泉。

乐观是一种信念，可以引领人们成就事业。假如心中没有希望，那就注定一事无成。在我们的祖先为美联邦建立基础的年代，是什么激励着他们去完成这个伟大任务，难道仅仅是对自由社会的憧憬吗？因为他们看到了希望的光芒在闪烁，所以他们不畏严寒和恶劣的天气，奋勇穿越茫茫雪原。面对希望的召唤，他们以坚强的信念努力奋斗，开山、填谷、铺路、架桥，把文明带向大地的每一个角落。虽然这些拓荒者们没有按照希伯来人的理想来建造这个世界，然而他们创造了经久不衰的社会模式，一直沿用到今天。他们给这片荒野带来了善于思考的心灵和必须遵守的法规，也带给了人们强烈的自治渴望，使这片荒野拥有了英国普通法——王子与庶民同罪，而我们社会的总体结构正是建立在这部法律基础之上。

更为重要的是，这部法律的制定有着积极乐观的根基。在拉丁国家的法庭，通常会有悲观消极的偏见出现，犯人在被证明无罪之前一般都会被视为有罪。而在英国和美国，态度则比较积极乐观，被告常常会被视为无罪，除非他再也无法否认他的罪行。据说在我们的法律体制下，许多罪犯都能被无罪释放，这显然要比让许多清白无辜的人蒙冤要好得多。

悲观的人哀叹道："人不可能一直拥有善，万事万物最终都会永久消亡，一切都将进入混沌状态。就算邪恶事物中曾有善的出现，那也是枉费工夫。世界在匆匆驶向毁灭的尽头。"但值得关注的是，作为世界上两个清醒理智、注重实用和遵纪守法的民族，英、美两国在法律上既承认人性善的一面，也没有回避各种关于人性恶的证据。

乐观是一种信念，可以引领人们走向成功。世界上的先知们都有一副好心肠，否则他们树立的旗帜只会孤零零地矗立在那里，没有一个护卫者。托尔斯泰的批评软弱无力，因为它们传递的是悲观的信息。假如他清楚地看到美国的缺点后依然相信她有能力克服一切，那么，我们的人民可能会从他的批评中受到鼓舞。

世界不会理会一个绝望的预言家，而是会驻足聆听爱默生的思想。他肯定了这个民族的诸多优秀品质，只对那些没有人能否认或为之辩驳的缺点加以批判。

这个世界也会聆听有着坚定意志的林肯的声音。在那个充满质疑、亟须援助的困难时代，他毫不退缩，坚信未来一定会成功，并以热切积极的希望激励整个民族。在充满绝望的黑夜里，他常说："一切都会好的！"他的信心使广大人民有了依靠，从而变得安定。像林肯这样的人如果提出批评，指出美国的缺点时，人民会服从他，会牢记他说的每一句话，但是对于耶利米[14]惯常的哀歌，人民的耳朵则变得麻木，不会加以理会。

我们的报纸应该牢记这一点，新闻报道仿佛现代社会的讲道坛，布道者决定了讲道的内容。要想让新闻报道在抗议各种不公行为时奏效，那么布道者在前九十九天里所说的话应该是欢快活泼、催人向上的。这样，在第一百天，他在说谴责的话时就会力量百倍。林肯采用的就是这种方式。他了解民众，充分信任他们，相信绝大多数人都拥有智慧和正义感。他说话直截了当，反应灵敏。"你不可能一直愚弄所有的人"，这句话表达了一个亘古不变的准则，教导我们要坚定不移地相信人性。

先知也希望获得荣耀，除非他是一个悲观的人。以赛亚[15]的种种预言令人心驰神往，力图帮助背井离乡的以色列子民重返家园。他的积极预言远比耶利米的哀歌要催人向上，后者只不过呼求把以色列的流放者从恶人手中解救出来。

人类是否还记得，即使是在主耶稣诞生的那天，他也是首先作为一个预示美好的使者来到人间的。他那满怀欢喜的乐观精神像甘泉一样滋润着干渴的嘴唇，他用无与伦比的语言为人类带来八种至高的祝福。[16]正是因为耶稣是一个乐观向上的人，他才一直主导西方世界这么多年。十九个世纪以来，全体基督徒都在注视着主耶稣神采奕奕的面庞，相信万物合力为善。圣保罗也曾教导我们，要在最艰难困苦的时候保持信仰，心存企盼，努力寻找上帝那无限的天国。一旦在那里领悟到完美，所有的缺陷与不足都会消融。

如果你天生是个盲人，那么就努力寻找黑暗赋予你的财富，它们比俄斐[17]的黄金更珍贵。它们是爱、美好、真理和希望，远比红宝石和蓝宝石珍贵。

主耶稣和圣保罗向我们传达了关于和平和理性的寓意，教导我们相信永恒的真理，相信上帝的爱，而不是相信物质世界，也不是相信武力征服。乐观的人能够明白，人类行为并不是受控于武装军队的指挥，而是服从道德力量的约束。亚历山大和拿破仑诉诸武力来征服世界，但比起牛顿、伽利略和圣奥古斯丁对世界无声的掌控，他们持续的时间非常短暂。可见，思想比烈火和利剑的威力更大。思想从一片国土传播到另一片国土，无声无息。人类走出自己的思想牢笼，获得了丰硕的收成，心里对上帝充满感激；相反，战场上的勇士所获得的成功仿佛他的帆布营地一样，"今天还是帐篷，而到了明天，全部被摧毁，消失得无影无踪，只剩下几个深坑和几堆稻草"。这是两千多年前耶稣的福音。耶稣诞生的日子是对乐观主义的欢呼和庆祝。

尽管还有很多邪魔恶鬼没有被征服，然而乐观的人并没有对此视而不见，相反，他信心百倍，充满希望。他的人生字典里没有沮丧这个词。他相信上帝的正义永存，人类永远不会丧失尊严。

　　历史记载了人类一直在胜利中前进，前进道路上的每一次停留只不过是下一次取得更大进步前的小憩。时代的发展是连续的，并没有从中间断开。假如我们祭拜的一些庙宇倒塌了，我们可以在神圣的遗址上建造起比原来更高大、更庄严的庙宇。假如我们在外形上看起来没有祖先那么英勇无畏，那么我们已经用一种高贵的精神取而代之，不再对敌人感到愤怒，而是给这些被我们征服的人包扎伤口。我们继承了人类过去所取得的所有成就，而且过去的很多梦想如今已变成活生生的现实。这一切体现了我们所坚守的希望和信念。

　　诚挚而纯粹的乐观主义精神光芒照耀着我，我脑海里在"未来的天幕上描绘了一幅更加辉煌的胜利画卷"。社会体制相互博弈，大国之间激烈竞争，我从争斗的混乱中看到了一个更光明的精神时代正在慢慢地出现，那里没有英国，没有法国，没有德国，没有美国，没有这个民族或那个民族；只有一个大家庭，那就是人类；只有一项法律，那就是和平；只有一种需求，那就是和谐；只有一种方式，那就是劳动；只有一个监督者，那就是上帝。

假如需要重新阐述乐观者的准则，我应该这样说："我相信上帝，相信人类，相信精神的力量。我相信鼓励自己和他人是一种神圣的职责；不说任何有损上帝世界的话，因为任何人都没有权利抱怨上帝造就的美好世界，况且成千上万的人一直在努力保持这样的美好世界。我坚信只有这样做，我们才能一步步靠近那个时代。到那时再不会出现这样的情形——一部分人生活安逸，而另一部分人却在经受煎熬。"这就是我发自内心的信念。

此外，还有一个信念就是乐观，一切皆取决于它。在每次经历暴风雨时要牢记这个信念，让它成为度过灾难和困苦的制胜法宝。乐观是人的心灵和宣称一切美好的上帝的精神之间的和谐与统一。

译 注

第一章 内在乐观

［1］威廉·威尔伯福斯（William Wilberforce，1759—1833），英国政治家，推动英国议会通过《废奴贸易法案》，为废奴事业奋斗终生。

［2］托马斯·卡莱尔（Thomas Carlyle，1795—1881），苏格兰散文家和历史学家。

［3］以上均为希腊神话和文学作品中人物，恩底弥翁（Endymion）是希腊神话中的月神，阿拉斯托尔（Alastor）是希腊神话中的复仇神，维特（Werther）则是德国著名作家哥德《少年维特之烦恼》中的人物，文中借此暗指法国大革命爆发后丧失行动力、变得绝望的那些人。

［4］约翰·理查德·格林（Jonh Richard Gveen，1837—1883），英国历史学家，著有《英国人民史》等作品。

第二章 外在乐观

[1] 贝内迪特·斯宾诺莎（Benedictus Spinoza，1632—1677），荷兰哲学家，西方近代哲学史中重要的理性主义者。

[2] 玛门，英文为 Mammon，古迦勒底语，意思是物质财富，在《圣经·新约》中使用，是钱的化身。

[3] 该演讲是尊敬的卡罗尔 D. 赖特于 1903 年 9 月在唯一神教派大会上发表的。

[4] 埃德蒙·伯克（Edmund Burke，1729—1797），西方 18 世纪重要政治家、哲学家，被视为英美保守主义的奠基者。

[5] 瓦朗坦·阿维（Valentin Haüy，1745—1822），法国翻译家、世界上第一所盲人学校的创办人，发明了一种将字母凸印以供盲人阅读的方法。

[6] 豪（Samuel Gridley Howe，1801—1876），盲人教育的积极倡导者，于 1829 年建立了美国的第一所盲人学校。

[7] 阿尔比派（Albigenses），公元 10 世纪由

鲍格米尔（Bogomil）创立，12 至 13 世纪流行于法国南部，其信徒谴责世俗，自称是纯洁的，被称为纯洁派教徒。

[8] 韦尔多派（Vaudois），约 1170 年出现于法国南部的一个基督教派别，16 世纪参加宗教改革运动。

[9] 莱辛（Gotthold Ephraim Lessing，1929—1981），德国作家、哲学家、剧作家、政论家和艺术评论家，启蒙运动时期最杰出的代表之一。

[10] 利奥十三世（Leo XIII），罗马天主教会第二百五十七位教皇，1878 年至 1903 年在位。

[11] 拉尔夫·沃尔多·爱默生（Ralph Waldo Emerson，1803—1882），美国著名作家、诗人、哲学家，美国超验主义运动的发起人。

[12] 威廉·埃勒里·钱宁（William Ellery Channing，1780—1842），美国基督教公理会自由派牧师、著作家，信奉上帝一位论，1825 年组成美国一位论协会，主张神学人文化，反对蓄奴、酗酒、贫困和战争。

第三章 践行乐观

[1] 阿图尔·叔本华（Arthur Schopenhauer，1788—1860），德国哲学家，其悲观主义对后世影响很大。

[2]《圣经·旧约·诗篇》中记载"我吃过炉灰，如同吃饭；我所喝的与眼泪掺杂"，作者引用炉灰代指生活中的苦难。作为虔诚的基督教徒，海伦·凯勒在该书中多处引用圣经典故，此为一例。

[3] 劳拉·布里奇曼（1829—1899），美国第一个学习语言并取得较大成就的盲聋人。

[4] 圣伯纳德（St. Bernard，1091—1153），法国修道士，罗马教皇顾问，西多会修道院生活秩序的主要缔造者。

[5] 圣约翰·鲍思高（St. John Bosco，1815—1888），意大利天主教牧师和教育家。

[6] 塞甘（Edward Seguin，1812—1880），法国精神病医生、弱智儿童教育家，以在法国和美国治疗认知缺陷的儿童而著称。

[7] 乔纳森·斯威夫特（Jonathan Swift，1667—1745），是英国启蒙运动中激进民主派的创始人，

18世纪英国最杰出的政论家和讽刺小说家，著有《格列佛游记》等作品。

[8] 萨克雷（William Makepeace Thackeray，1811—1863），19世纪英国重要作家，著有《名利场》等作品。

[9] 奥马尔·海亚姆（Omar Khayyám，1048—1132），著名的波斯数学家、诗人、天文学家、哲学家。《鲁拜集》，*Rubáiyát*，亦称"柔巴伊"，阿拉伯语的意思是"四行诗"。1859年，英国学者兼诗人爱德华·菲茨杰拉德翻译并改写了该诗集，出版后对英语世界文学产生重大影响，被列为世界必读五十本书籍中的信仰类首本。

[10] 罗伯特·勃朗宁（Robert Browning，1812—1889），英国维多利亚时期代表诗人之一。

[11] 罗伯特·路易斯·斯蒂文森（Robert Louis Stevenson，1850—1894），英国小说家、诗人和随笔作家。

[12] 塞缪尔·约翰逊（Samuel Johnson，1709—1784），英国作家、批评家，英国文学史上重要的诗人、散文家、传记家，其编纂的《词典》对英语发展作出了重大贡献。

[13] 查尔斯·兰姆（Charles Lamb，1775—1834），英国散之文家。

[14] 耶利米（Jeremiah），犹太国最黑暗时期的先知，《圣经·旧约·耶利米哀歌》中主要记载了耶利米的言行。

[15] 以赛亚（Isaiah），古以色列战乱时代的大先知，见《圣经·旧约·以赛亚书》。

[16]《圣经·新约·马太福音》中，记载了耶稣基督宣讲的八福，也被称为"山上宝训"，被认为是基督教徒言行的基本准则。

[17] 俄斐（Ophir），见《圣经·列王记》，是盛产黄金和宝石之地。

My Key of Life

To My Teacher

Publisher's Note

My Key of Life is long philosophical essay by the distinguished American blind-deaf writer, Helen Keller. She wrote it before she would graduate from Radcliffe College soon. It was first published as *Optimism* in 1903, and then reprinted as *My Key of Life*, *Optimism* as well as *The Practice of Optimism*. It was also published together with Helen Keller's other works.

In viewing of its contents and the publishing form of both Chinese and English, it is decided to publish this essay independently and use the name *My Key of Life*.

It has been more than one century since Helen Keller wrote this famous philosophical essay. Social environment and time background have already been greatly changed. A few paragraphs in the essay seem to be difficult to understand today. Therefore, such paragraphs have been appropriately omitted in this edition.

CONTENTS

Publisher's Note

Part I Optimism Within ·················· (61)

My optimism is grounded in two worlds, myself and what is about me. I demand that the world be good, and lo, it obeys. I proclaim the world good, and facts range themselves to prove my proclamation overwhelmingly true.

Part II Optimism Without ·················· (73)

All the world's great philosophers have been lovers of God and believers in man's inner goodness. To know the history of philosophy is to know that the highest thinkers of the ages, the seers of the tribes and the nations, have been optimists.

Part III The Practice of Optimism .... (97)

Optimism compels the world forward, and pessimism retards it. Optimism is the faith that leads to achievement; nothing can be done without hope.

Part I Optimism Within

My optimism is grounded in two worlds, myself and what is about me. I demand that the world be good, and lo, it obeys. I proclaim the world good, and facts range themselves to prove my proclamation overwhelmingly true.

COULD we choose our environment, and were desire in human undertakings synonymous with endowment, all men would, I suppose, be optimists. Certainly most of us regard happiness as the proper end of all earthly enterprise. The will to be happy animates alike the philosopher, the prince and the chimney-sweep. No matter how dull, or how mean, or how wise a man is, he feels that happiness is his indisputable right.

It is curious to observe what different ideals of happiness people cherish, and in what singular places they look for this well-spring of their life. Many look for it in the hoarding of riches, some in the pride of power, and others in the achievements of art and literature; a few seek it in the exploration of their own minds, or in the search for knowledge.

Most people measure their happiness in terms of physical pleasure and material possession. Could they win some visible goal which they have set on the horizon, how happy they would be! Lacking this gift or that circumstance, they would be miserable. If happiness is to be so measured, I who cannot hear or see have every reason to sit in a corner with folded hands and weep.

If I am happy in spite of my deprivations, if my happiness is so deep that it is a faith, so thoughtful that it becomes a philosophy of life, — if, in short, I am an optimist, my testimony to the creed of optimism is worth hearing. As sinners stand up in meeting and testify to the goodness of God, so one who is called afflicted may rise up in gladness of conviction and testify to the goodness of life.

Once I knew the depth where no hope was, and darkness lay on the face of all things. Then love came and set my soul free. Once I knew only darkness and stillness. Now I know hope and joy.

Once I fretted and beat myself against the wall that shut me in. Now I rejoice in the consciousness that I can think, act and attain heaven. My life was without past or future; death, the pessimist would say, "a consummation devoutly to be wished."

But a little word from the fingers of another fell into my hand that clutched at emptiness, and my heart leaped to the rapture of living. Night fled before the day of thought, and love and joy and hope came up in a passion of obedience to knowledge. Can any one who has escaped such captivity, who has felt the thrill and glory of freedom, be a pessimist?

My early experience was thus a leap from bad to good. If I tried, I could not check the momentum of my first leap out of the dark; to move breast forward is a habit learned suddenly at that first moment of release and rush into the light. With the first word I used intelligently, I learned to live, to think, to hope. Darkness cannot shut me in again. I have had a glimpse of the shore, and can now live by the hope of reaching it.

So my optimism is no mild and unreasoning satisfaction. A poet once said I must be happy because I did not see the bare, cold present, but lived in a beautiful dream. I do live in a beautiful dream; but that dream is the actual, the present, —not cold, but warm; not bare, but furnished with a thousand blessings. The very evil which the poet supposed would be a cruel disillusionment is necessary to the fullest knowledge of joy. Only by contact with evil could I have learned to feel by contrast the beauty of truth and love and goodness.

It is a mistake always to contemplate the good and ignore the evil, because by making people neglectful it lets in disaster. There is a dangerous optimism of ignorance and indifference. It is not enough to say that the twentieth century is the best age in the history of mankind, and to take refuge from the evils of the world in skyey dreams of good. How many good men, prosperous and contented, looked around and saw naught but good, while millions of their fellowmen were bartered and sold like cattle! No doubt, there were comfortable optimists who thought Wilberforce a meddlesome fanatic when he was working with might and main to free the slaves.

I distrust the rash optimism in this country that cries, "Hurrah, we're all right! This is the greatest nation on earth," when there are grievances that call loudly for redress. That is false optimism. Optimism that does not count the cost is like a house builded on sand. A man must understand evil and be acquainted with sorrow before he can write himself an optimist and expect others to believe that he has reason for the faith that is in him.

I know what evil is. Once or twice I have wrestled with it, and for a time felt its chilling touch on my life; so I speak with knowledge when I say that evil is of no consequence, except as a sort of mental gymnastic. For the very reason that I have come in contact with it, I am more truly an optimist. I can say with conviction that the struggle which evil necessitates is one of the greatest blessings. It makes us strong, patient, helpful men and women. It lets us into the soul of things and teaches us that although the world is full of suffering, it is full also of the overcoming of it.

My optimism, then, does not rest on the absence of evil, but on a glad belief in the preponderance of good and a willing effort always to cooperate with the good, that it may prevail. I try to increase the power God has given me to see the best in everything and every one, and make that Best a part of my life. The world is sown with good; but unless I turn my glad thoughts into practical living and till my own field, I cannot reap a kernel of the good.

Thus my optimism is grounded in two worlds, myself and what is about me. I demand that the world be good, and lo, it obeys. I proclaim the world good, and facts range themselves to prove my proclamation overwhelmingly true. To what is good I open the doors of my being, and jealously shut them against what is bad. Such is the force of this beautiful and wilful conviction, it carries itself in the face of all opposition. I am never discouraged by absence of good. I never can be argued into hopelessness. Doubt and mistrust are the mere panic of timid imagination, which the steadfast heart will conquer, and the large mind transcend.

As my college days draw to a close, I find myself looking forward with beating heart and bright anticipations to what the future holds of activity for me. My share in the work of the world may be limited; but the fact that it is work makes it precious. Nay, the desire and will to work is optimism itself.

Two generations ago Carlyle flung forth his gospel of work. To the dreamers of the Revolution, who built cloud-castles of happiness, and, when the inevitable winds rent the castles asunder, turned pessimists—to those ineffectual Endymions, Alastors and Werthers, this Scots peasant, man of dreams in the hard, practical world, cried aloud his creed of labor. "Be no longer a Chaos, but a World. Produce! Produce! Were it but the pitifullest infinitesimal fraction of a product, produce it, in God's name! 'T is the utmost thou hast in thee; out with it, then. Up, up! whatsoever thy hand findeth to do, do it with thy whole might. Work while it is called Today; for the Night cometh wherein no man may work."

Some have said Carlyle was taking refuge from a hard world by bidding men grind and toil, eyes to the earth, and so forget their misery. This is not Carlyle's thought. "Fool!" he cries, "the Ideal is in thyself; the Impediment is also in thyself. Work out the Ideal in the poor, miserable Actual; live, think, believe, and be free!" It is plain what he says, that work, production, brings life out of chaos, makes the individual a world, an order; and order is optimism.

I, too, can work, and because I love to labor with my head and my hands, I am an optimist in spite of all. I used to think I should be thwarted in my desire to do something useful. But I have found out that though the ways in which I can make myself useful are few, yet the work open to me is endless.

The gladdest laborer in the vineyard may be a cripple. Even should the others outstrip him, yet the vineyard ripens in the sun each year, and the full clusters weigh into his hand.

Darwin could work only half an hour at a time; yet in many diligent half-hours he laid anew the foundations of philosophy.

I long to accomplish a great and noble task; but it is my chief duty and joy to accomplish humble tasks as though they were great and noble. It is my service to think how I can best fulfil the demands that each day makes upon me, and to rejoice that others can do what I cannot.

Green, the historian,[1] tells us that the world is moved along, not only by the mighty shoves of its heroes, but also by the aggregate of the tiny pushes of each honest worker; and that thought alone suffices to guide me in this dark world and wide. I love the good that others do; for their activity is an assurance that whether I can help or not, the true and the good will stand sure.

---

[1] *Life and Letters of John Richard Green.* Edited by Leslie Stephen.

I trust, and nothing that happens disturbs my trust. I recognize the beneficence of the power which we all worship as supreme—Order, Fate, the Great Spirit, Nature, God. I recognize this power in the sun that makes all things grow and keeps life afoot. I make a friend of this indefinable force, and straightway I feel glad, brave and ready for any lot Heaven may decree for me. This is my religion of optimism.

Part II Optimism Without

All the world's great philo-sophers have been lovers of God and believers in man's inner goodness. To know the history of philo-sophy is to know that the highest thinkers of the ages, the seers of the tribes and the nations, have been optimists.

OPTIMISM, then, is a fact within my own heart. But as I look out upon life, my heart meets no contradiction. The outward world justifies my inward universe of good. All through the years I have spent in college, my reading has been a continuous discovery of good. In literature, philosophy, religion and history I find the mighty witnesses to my faith.

Philosophy is the history of a deafblind person writ large. From the talks of Socrates up through Plato, Berkeley and Kant, philosophy records the efforts of human intelligence to be free of the clogging material world and fly forth into a universe of pure idea.

A deaf-blind person ought to find special meaning in Plato's Ideal World. These things which you see and hear and touch are not the reality of realities, but imperfect manifestations of the Idea, the Principle, the Spiritual; the Idea is the truth, the rest is delusion.

If this be so, my brethren who enjoy the fullest use of the senses are not aware of any reality which may not equally well be in reach of my mind. Philosophy gives to the mind the prerogative of seeing truth, and bears us into a realm where I, who am blind, am not different from you who see.

When I learned from Berkeley that your eyes receive an inverted image of things which your brain unconsciously corrects, I began to suspect that the eye is not a very reliable instrument after all, and I felt as one who had been restored to equality with others, glad, not because the senses avail them so little, but because in God's eternal world, mind and spirit avail so much.

It seemed to me that philosophy had been written for my special consolation, whereby I get even with some modern philosophers who apparently think that I was intended as an experimental case for their special instruction! But in a little measure my small voice of individual experience does join in the declaration of philosophy that the good is the only world, and that world is a world of spirit. It is also a universe where order is All, where an unbroken logic holds the parts together, where disorder defines itself as non-existence, where evil, as St. Augustine held, is delusion, and therefore is not.

The meaning of philosophy to me is not only in its principles, but also in the happy isolation of its great expounders. They were seldom of the world, even when like Plato and Leibnitz they moved in its courts and drawing-rooms. To the tumult of life they were deaf, and they were blind to its distraction and perplexing diversities. Sitting alone, but not in darkness, they learned to find everything in themselves, and failing to find it even there, they still trusted in meeting the truth face to face when they should leave the earth behind and become partakers in the wisdom of God. The great mystics lived alone, deaf and blind, but dwelling with God.

I understand how it was possible for Spinoza to find deep and sustained happiness when he was excommunicated, poor, despised and suspected alike by Jew and Christian; not that the kind world of men ever treated me so, but that his isolation from the universe of sensuous joys is somewhat analogous to mine. He loved the good for its own sake. Like many great spirits he accepted his place in the world, and confided himself childlike to a higher power, believing that it worked through his hands and predominated in his being. He trusted implicitly, and that is what I do.

Deep, solemn optimism, it seems to me, should spring from this firm belief in the presence of God in the individual; not a remote, unapproachable governor of the universe, but a God who is very near every one of us, who is present not only in earth, sea and sky, but also in every pure and noble impulse of our hearts, "the source and centre of all minds, their only point of rest."

Thus from philosophy I learn that we see only shadows and know only in part, and that all things change; but the mind, the unconquerable mind, compasses all truth, embraces the universe as it is, converts the shadows to realities and makes tumultuous changes seem but moments in an eternal silence, or short lines in the infinite theme of perfection, and the evil but "a halt on the way to good."

Though with my hand I grasp only a small part of the universe, with my spirit I see the whole, and in my thought I can compass the beneficent laws by which it is governed. The confidence and trust which these conceptions inspire teach me to rest safe in my life as in a fate, and protect me from spectral doubts and fears. Verily, blessed are ye that have not seen, and yet have believed.

All the world's great philosophers have been lovers of God and believers in man's inner goodness. To know the history of philosophy is to know that the highest thinkers of the ages, the seers of the tribes and the nations, have been optimists.

The growth of philosophy is the story of man's spiritual life. Outside lies that great mass of events which we call History. As I look on this mass, I see it take form and shape itself in the ways of God. The history of man is an epic of progress. In the world within and the world without I see a wonderful correspondence, a glorious symbolism which reveals the human and the divine communing together, the lesson of philosophy repeated in fact. In all the parts that compose the history of mankind hides the spirit of good, and gives meaning to the whole.

Far back in the twilight of history I see the savage fleeing from the forces of nature which he has not learned to control, and seeking to propitiate supernatural beings which are but the creation of his superstitious fear. With a shift of imagination I see the savage emancipated, civilized. He no longer worships the grim deities of ignorance. Through suffering he has learned to build a roof over his head, to defend his life and his home, and over his state he has erected a temple in which he worships the joyous gods of light and song. From suffering he has learned justice; from the struggle with his fellows he has learned the distinction between right and wrong which makes him a moral being. He is gifted with the genius of Greece.

But Greece was not perfect. Her poetical and religious ideals were far above her practice; therefore she died, that her ideals might survive to ennoble coming ages.

Rome, too, left the world a rich inheritance. Through the vicissitudes of history her laws and ordered government have stood a majestic object-lesson for the ages. But when the stern, frugal character of her people ceased to be the bone and sinew of her civilization, Rome fell.

Then came the new nations of the North and founded a more permanent society. The base of Greek and Roman society was the slave, crushed into the condition of the wretches who "labored, foredone, in the field and at the workshop, like haltered horses, if blind, so much the quieter." The base of the new society was the freeman who fought, tilled, judged and grew from more to more. He wrought a state out of tribal kinship and fostered an independence and self-reliance which no oppression could destroy. The story of man's slow ascent from savagery through barbarism and self-mastery to civilization is the embodiment of the spirit of optimism. From the first hour of the new nations each century has seen a better Europe, until the development of the world demanded America.

Tolstoi said the other day that America, once the hope of the world, was in bondage to Mammon. Tolstoi and other Europeans have still much to learn about this great, free country of ours before they understand the unique civic struggle which America is undergoing. She is confronted with the mighty task of assimilating all the foreigners that are drawn together from every country, and welding them into one people with one national spirit. We have the right to demand the forbearance of critics until the United States has demonstrated whether she can make one people out of all the nations of the earth.

London economists are alarmed at less than five hundred thousand foreign-born in a population of six million, and discuss earnestly the danger of too many aliens. But what is their problem in comparison with that of New York, which counts near-ly one million five hundred thousand foreigners among its three and a half million citizens? Think of it! Every third person in our American metropolis is an alien. By these figures alone America's greatness can be measured.

It is true, America has devoted herself largely to the solution of material problems—breaking the fields, opening mines, irrigating deserts, spanning the continent with railroads; but she is doing these things in a new way, by educating her people, by placing at the service of every man's need every resource of human skill. She is transmuting her industrial wealth into the education of her workmen, so that unskilled people shall have no place in American life, so that all men shall bring mind and soul to the control of matter. Her children are not drudges and slaves. The Constitution has declared it, and the spirit of our institutions has confirmed it. The best the land can teach them they shall know. They shall learn that there is no upper class in their country, and no lower, and they shall understand how it is that God and His world are for everybody.

America might do all this, and still be selfish, still be a worshipper of Mammon. But America is the home of charity as well as of commerce. In the midst of roaring traffic, side by side with noisy factory and sky-reaching warehouse, one sees the school, the library, the hospital, the park—works of public benevolence which represent wealth wrought into ideas that shall endure forever. Behold what America has already done to alleviate suffering and restore the afflicted to society—given sight to the fingers of the blind, language to the dumb lip, and mind to the idiot clay, and tell me if indeed she worships Mammon only. Who shall measure the sympathy, skill and intelligence with which she ministers to all who come to her, and lessens the ever-swelling tide of poverty, misery and degradation which every year rolls against her gates from all the nations?

When I reflect on all these facts, I cannot but think that, Tolstoi and other theorists to the contrary, it is a splendid thing to be an American. In America the optimist finds abundant reason for confidence in the present and hope for the future, and this hope, this confidence, may well extend over all the great nations of the earth.

If we compare our own time with the past, we find in modern statistics a solid foundation for a confident and buoyant world-optimism. Beneath the doubt, the unrest, the materialism, which surround us still glows and burns at the world's best life a steadfast faith. To hear the pessimist, one would think civilization had bivouacked in the Middle Ages, and had not had marching orders since. He does not realize that the progress of evolution is not an uninterrupted march.

"Now touching goal, now backward hurl'd,

Toils the indomitable world."

I have recently read an address by one whose knowledge it would be presumptuous to challenge.[1] In it I find abundant evidence of progress.

During the past fifty years crime has decreased. True, the records of today contain a longer list of crime. But our statistics are more complete and accurate than the statistics of times past. Besides, there are many offences on the list which half a century ago would not have been thought of as crimes. This shows that the public conscience is more sensitive than it ever was.

Our definition of crime has grown stricter, our punishment of it more lenient and intelligent. The old feeling of revenge has largely disappeared. It is no longer an eye for an eye, a tooth for a tooth.

---

[1] Address by the Hon. Carroll D. Wright before the Unitarian Conference, September, 1903.

The criminal is treated as one who is diseased. He is confined not merely for punishment, but because he is a menace to society. While he is under restraint, he is treated with humane care and disciplined so that his mind shall be cured of its disease, and he shall be restored to society able to do his part of its work.

Another sign of awakened and enlightened public conscience is the effort to provide the working-class with better houses. Did it occur to any one a hundred years ago to think whether the dwellings of the poor were sanitary, convenient or sunny? Do not forget that in the "good old times" cholera and typhus devastated whole counties, and that pestilence walked abroad in the capitals of Europe.

Not only have our laboring-classes better houses and better places to work in; but employers recognize the right of the employed to seek more than the bare wage of existence. In the darkness and turmoil of our modern industrial strifes we discern but dimly the principles that underlie the struggle. The recognition of the right of all men to life, liberty and the pursuit of happiness, a spirit of conciliation such as Burke dreamed of, the willingness on the part of the strong to make concessions to the weak, the realization that the rights of the employer are bound up in the rights of the employed—in these the optimist beholds the signs of our times.

Another right which the State has recognized as belonging to each man is the right to an education. In the enlightened parts of Europe and in America every city, every town, every village, has its school; and it is no longer a class who have access to knowledge, for to the children of the poorest laborer the school-door stands open. From the civilized nations universal education is driving the dull host of illiteracy.

Education broadens to include all men, and deepens to reach all truths. Scholars are no longer confined to Greek, Latin and mathematics, but they also study science; and science converts the dreams of the poet, the theory of the mathematician and the fiction of the economist into ships, hospitals and instruments that enable one skilled hand to perform the work of a thousand. The student of today is not asked if he has learned his grammar. Is he a mere grammar-machine, a dry catalogue of scientific facts, or has he acquired the qualities of manliness? His supreme lesson is to grapple with great public questions, to keep his mind hospitable to new ideas and new views of truth, to restore the finer ideals that are lost sight of in the struggle for wealth and to promote justice between man and man. He learns that there may be substitutes for human labor—horse-power and machinery and books; but "there are no substitutes for common sense, patience, integrity, courage."

Who can doubt the vastness of the achievements of education when one considers how different the condition of the blind and the deaf is from what it was a century ago? They were then objects of superstitious pity, and shared the lowest beggar's lot. Everybody looked upon their case as hopeless, and this view plunged them deeper in despair. The blind themselves laughed in the face of Haüy when he offered to teach them to read. How pitiable is the cramped sense of imprisonment in circumstances which teaches men to expect no good and to treat any attempt to relieve them as the vagary of a disordered mind! But now, behold the transformation; see how institutions and industrial establishments for the blind have sprung up as if by magic; see how many of the deaf have learned not only to read and write, but to speak; and remember that the faith and patience of Dr. Howe have borne fruit in the efforts that are being made everywhere to educate the deaf-blind and equip them for the struggle. Do you wonder that I am full of hope and lifted up?

The highest result of education is tolerance. Long ago men fought and died for their faith; but it took ages to teach them the other kind of courage—the courage to recognize the faiths of their brethren and their rights of conscience. Tolerance is the first principle of community; it is the spirit which conserves the best that all men think. No loss by flood and lightning, no destruction of cities and temples by the hostile forces of nature, has deprived man of so many noble lives and impulses as those which his intolerance has destroyed.

With wonder and sorrow I go back in thought to the ages of intolerance and bigotry. I see Jesus received with scorn and nailed on the cross. I see his followers hounded and tortured and burned. I am present where the finer spirits that revolt from the superstition of the Middle Ages are accused of impiety and stricken down. I behold the children of Israel reviled and persecuted unto death by those who pretend Christianity with the tongue; I see them driven from land to land, hunted from refuge to refuge, summoned to the felon's place, exposed to the whip, mocked as they utter amid the pain of martyrdom a confession of the faith which they have kept with such splendid constancy. The same bigotry that oppresses the Jews falls tiger-like upon Christian nonconformists of purest lives and wipes out the Albigenses and the peaceful Vaudois, "whose bones lie on the mountains cold."

I see the clouds part slowly, and I hear a cry of protest against the bigot. The restraining hand of tolerance is laid upon the inquisitor, and the humanist utters a message of peace to the persecuted. Instead of the cry, "Burn the heretic!" men study the human soul with sympathy, and there enters into their hearts a new reverence for that which is unseen.

The idea of brotherhood redawns upon the world with a broader significance than the narrow association of members in a sect or creed; and thinkers of great soul like Lessing challenge the world to say which is more godlike, the hatred and tooth-and-nail grapple of conflicting religions, or sweet accord and mutual helpfulness.

Ancient prejudice of man against his brother-man wavers and retreats before the radiance of a more generous sentiment, which will not sacrifice men to forms, or rob them of the comfort and strength they find in their own beliefs. The heresy of one age becomes the orthodoxy of the next. Mere tolerance has given place to a sentiment of brotherhood between sincere men of all denominations. The optimist rejoices in the affectionate sympathy between Catholic heart and Protestant heart which finds a gratifying expression in the universal respect and warm admiration for Leo XIII on the part of good men the world over. The centenary celebrations of the births of Emerson and Channing are beautiful examples of the tribute which men of all creeds pay to the memory of a pure soul.

Thus in my outlook upon our times I find that I am glad to be a citizen of the world, and as I regard my country, I find that to be an American is to be an optimist. I know the unhappy and unrighteous story of what has been done in the Philippines beneath our flag; but I believe that in the accidents of statecraft the best intelligence of the people sometimes fails to express itself.

I read in the history of Julius Cæsar that during the civil wars there were millions of peaceful herdsmen and laborers who worked as long as they could, and fled before the advance of the armies that were led by the few, then waited until the danger was past, and returned to repair damages with patient hands. So the people are patient and honest, while their rulers stumble.

I rejoice to see in the world and in this country a new and better patriotism than that which seeks the life of an enemy. It is a patriotism higher than that of the battle-field. It moves thousands to lay down their lives in social service, and every life so laid down brings us a step nearer the time when corn-fields shall no more be fields of battle. So when I heard of the cruel fighting in the Philippines, I did not despair, because I knew that the hearts of our people were not in that fight, and that sometime the hand of the destroyer must be stayed.

Part III The Practice of Optimism

Optimism compels the world forward, and pessimism retards it. Optimism is the faith that leads to achievement; nothing can be done without hope.

THE test of all beliefs is their practical effect in life. If it be true that optimism compels the world forward, and pessimism retards it, then it is dangerous to propagate a pessimistic philosophy. One who believes that the pain in the world outweighs the joy, and expresses that unhappy conviction, only adds to the pain.

Schopenhauer is an enemy to the race. Even if he earnestly believed that this is the most wretched of possible worlds, he should not promulgate a doctrine which robs men of the incentive to fight with circumstance. If Life gave him ashes for bread, it was his fault. Life is a fair field, and the right will prosper if we stand by our guns.

Let pessimism once take hold of the mind, and life is all topsy-turvy, all vanity and vexation of spirit. There is no cure for individual or social disorder, except in forgetfulness and annihilation.

"Let us eat, drink and be merry," says the pessimist, "for tomorrow we die." If I regarded my life from the point of view of the pessimist, I should be undone. I should seek in vain for the light that does not visit my eyes and the music that does not ring in my ears. I should beg night and day and never be satisfied. I should sit apart in awful solitude, a prey to fear and despair. But since I consider it a duty to myself and to others to be happy, I escape a misery worse than any physical deprivation.

Who shall dare let his incapacity for hope or goodness cast a shadow upon the courage of those who bear their burdens as if they were privileges? The optimist cannot fall back, cannot falter; for he knows his neighbor will be hindered by his failure to keep in line. He will therefore hold his place fearlessly and remember the duty of silence. Sufficient unto each heart is its own sorrow. He will take the iron claws of circumstance in his hand and use them as tools to break away the obstacles that block his path. He will work as if upon him alone depended the establishment of heaven on earth.

We have seen that the world's philosophers—the Sayers of the Word—were optimists; so also are the men of action and achievement—the Doers of the Word. Dr. Howe found his way to Laura Bridgman's soul because he began with the belief that he could reach it. English jurists had said that the deaf-blind were idiots in the eyes of the law. Behold what the optimist does. He controverts a hard legal axiom; he looks behind the dull impassive clay and sees a human soul in bondage, and quietly, resolutely sets about its deliverance. His efforts are victorious. He creates intelligence out of idiocy and proves to the law that the deaf-blind man is a responsible being.

When Haüy offered to teach the blind to read, he was met by pessimism that laughed at his folly.

Had he not believed that the soul of man is mightier than the ignorance that fetters it, had he not been an optimist, he would not have turned the fingers of the blind into new instruments. No pessimist ever discovered the secrets of the stars, or sailed to an uncharted land, or opened a new heaven to the human spirit.

St. Bernard was so deeply an optimist that he believed two hundred and fifty enlightened men could illuminate the darkness which overwhelmed the period of the Crusades; and the light of his faith broke like a new day upon western Europe.

John Bosco, the benefactor of the poor and the friendless of Italian cities, was another optimist, another prophet who, perceiving a Divine Idea while it was yet afar, proclaimed it to his countrymen. Although they laughed at his vision and called him a madman, yet he worked on patiently, and with the labor of his hands he maintained a

101

home for little street waifs. In the fervor of enthusiasm he predicted the wonderful movement which should result from his work. Even in the days before he had money or patronage, he drew glowing pictures of the splendid system of schools and hospitals which should spread from one end of Italy to the other, and he lived to see the organization of the San Salvador Society, which was the embodiment of his prophetic optimism.

When Dr. Seguin declared his opinion that the feeble-minded could be taught, again people laughed, and in their complacent wisdom said he was no better than an idiot himself. But the noble optimist persevered, and by and by the reluctant pessimists saw that he whom they ridiculed had become one of the world's philanthropists.

Thus the optimist believes, attempts, achieves. He stands always in the sunlight. Some day the wonderful, the inexpressible, arrives and shines upon him, and he is there to welcome it. His soul meets his own and beats a glad march to every new discovery, every fresh victory over difficulties, every addition to human knowledge and happiness.

We have found that our great philosophers and our great men of action are optimists. So, too, our most potent men of letters have been optimists in their books and in their lives. No pessimist ever won an audience commensurately wide with his genius, and many optimistic writers have been read and admired out of all measure to their talents, simply because they wrote of the sunlit side of life.

Dickens, Lamb, Goldsmith, Irving, all the well-beloved and gentle humorists, were optimists. Swift, the pessimist, has never had as many readers as his towering genius should command, and indeed, when he comes down into our century and meets Thackeray, that generous optimist can hard-ly do him justice.

In spite of the latter-day notoriety of the "Rubáiyát" of Omar Khayyám, we may set it down as a rule that he who would be heard must be a believer, must have a fundamental optimism in his philosophy. He may bluster and disagree and lament as Carlyle and Ruskin do sometimes; but a basic confidence in the good destiny of life and of the world must underlie his work.

Shakespeare is the prince of optimists. His tragedies are a revelation of moral order. In "Lear" and "Hamlet" there is a looking forward to something better, some one is left at the end of the play to right wrong, restore society and build the state anew. The later plays, "The Tempest" and "Cymbeline," show a beautiful, placid optimism which delights in reconciliations and reunions and which plans for the triumph of external as well as internal good.

If Browning were less difficult to read, he would surely be the dominant poet in this century. I feel the ecstasy with which he exclaims, "Oh, good gigantic smile o' the brown old earth this autumn morning!" And how he sets my brain going when he says, because there is imperfection, there must be perfection; completeness must come of incompleteness; failure is an evidence of triumph for the fulness of the days. Yes, discord is, that harmony may be; pain destroys, that health may renew; perhaps I am deaf and blind that others likewise afflicted may see and hear with a more perfect sense! From Browning I learn that there is no lost good, and that makes it easier for me to go at life, right or wrong, do the best I know, and fear not. My heart responds proudly to his exhortation to pay gladly life's debt of pain, darkness and cold. Lift up your burden, it is God's gift, bear it nobly.

The man of letters whose voice is to prevail must be an optimist, and his voice often learns its message from his life. Stevenson's life has become a tradition only ten years after his death; he has taken his place among the heroes, the bravest man of letters since Johnson and Lamb. I remember an hour when I was discouraged and ready to falter. For days I had been pegging away at a task which refused to get itself accomplished. In the midst of my perplexity I read an essay of Stevenson which made me feel as if I had been "outing" in the sunshine, instead of losing heart over a difficult task. I tried again with new courage and succeeded almost before I knew it. I have failed many times since; but I have never felt so disheartened as I did before that sturdy preacher gave me my lesson in the "fashion of the smiling face."

Read Schopenhauer and Omar, and you will grow to find the world as hollow as they find it.

Read Green's history of England, and the world is peopled with heroes. I never knew why

Green's history thrilled me with the vigor of romance until I read his biography. Then I learned how his quick imagination transfigured the hard, bare facts of life into new and living dreams. When he and his wife were too poor to have a fire, he would sit before the unlit hearth and pretend that it was ablaze. "Drill your thoughts," he said; "shut out the gloomy and call in the bright. There is more wisdom in shutting one's eyes than your copybook philosophers will allow."

Every optimist moves along with progress and hastens it, while every pessimist would keep the world at a standstill. The consequence of pessimism in the life of a nation is the same as in the life of the individual. Pessimism kills the instinct that urges men to struggle against poverty, ignorance and crime, and dries up all the fountains of joy in the world.

Optimism is the faith that leads to achievement; nothing can be done without hope. When our forefathers laid the foundation of the American commonwealths, what nerved them to their task but a vision of a free community? Against the cold, inhospitable sky, across the wilderness white with snow, where lurked the hidden savage, gleamed the bow of promise, toward which they set their faces with the faith that levels mountains, fills up valleys, bridges rivers and carries civilization to the uttermost parts of the earth. Although the pioneers could not build according to the Hebraic ideal they saw, yet they gave the pattern of all that is most enduring in our country today. They brought to the wilderness the thinking mind, the printed book, the deep-rooted desire for self-government and the English common law that judges alike the king and the subject, the law on which rests the whole structure of our society.

It is significant that the foundation of that law is optimistic. In Latin countries the court proceeds with a pessimistic bias. The prisoner is held guilty until he is proved innocent. In England and the United States there is an optimistic presumption that the accused is innocent until it is no longer possible to deny his guilt. Under our system, it is said, many criminals are acquitted; but it is surely better so than that many innocent persons should suffer.

The pessimist cries, "There is no enduring good in man! The tendency of all things is through perpetual loss to chaos in the end. If there was ever an idea of good in things evil, it was impotent, and the world rushes on to ruin." But behold, the law of the two most sober-minded, practical and law-abiding nations on earth assumes the good in man and demands a proof of the bad.

Optimism is the faith that leads to achievement. The prophets of the world have been of good heart, or their standards would have stood naked in the field without a defender. Tolstoi's strictures lose power because they are pessimistic. If he had seen clearly the faults of America, and still believed in her capacity to overcome them, our people might have felt the stimulation of his censure.

But the world turns its back on a hopeless prophet and listens to Emerson who takes into account the best qualities of the nation and attacks only the vices which no one can defend or deny.

It listens to the strong man, Lincoln, who in times of doubt, trouble and need does not falter. He sees success afar, and by strenuous hope, by hoping against hope, inspires a nation. Through the night of despair he says, "All is well," and thousands rest in his confidence. When such a man censures, and points to a fault, the nation obeys, and his words sink into the ears of men; but to the lamentations of the habitual Jeremiah the ear grows dull.

Our newspapers should remember this. The

press is the pulpit of the modern world, and on the preachers who fill it much depends. If the protest of the press against unrighteous measures is to avail, then for ninetynine days the word of the preacher should be buoyant and of good cheer, so that on the hundredth day the voice of censure may be a hundred times strong. This was Lincoln's way. He knew the people; he believed in them and rested his faith on the justice and wisdom of the great majority. When in his rough and ready way he said, "You can't fool all the people all the time," he expressed a great principle, the doctrine of faith in human nature.

The prophet is not without honor, save he be a pessimist. The ecstatic prophecies of Isaiah did far more to restore the exiles of Israel to their homes than the lamentations of Jeremiah did to deliver them from the hands of evil-doers.

Even on Christmas Day do men remember that

Christ came as a prophet of good? His joyous optimism is like water to feverish lips, and has for its highest expression the eight beatitudes. It is because Christ is an optimist that for ages he has dominated the Western world. For nineteen centuries Christendom has gazed into his shining face and felt that all things work together for good. St. Paul, too, taught the faith which looks beyond the hardest things into the infinite horizon of heaven, where all limitations are lost in the light of perfect understanding.

If you are born blind, search the treasures of darkness. They are more precious than the gold of Ophir. They are love and goodness and truth and hope, and their price is above rubies and sapphires.

Jesus utters and Paul proclaims a message of peace and a message of reason, a belief in the Idea, not in things, in love, not in conquest. The optimist is he who sees that men's actions are directed not by squadrons and armies, but by moral power, that the conquests of Alexander and Napoleon are less abiding than Newton's and Galileo's and St. Augustine's silent mastery of the world. Ideas are mightier than fire and sword. Noiselessly they propagate themselves from land to land, and mankind goes out and reaps the rich harvest and thanks God; but the achievements of the warrior are like his canvas city, "today a camp, tomorrow all struck and vanished, a few pit-holes and heaps of straw." This was the gospel of Jesus two thousand years ago. Christmas Day is the festival of optimism.

Although there are still great evils which have not been subdued, and the optimist is not blind to them, yet he is full of hope. Despondency has no place in his creed, for he believes in the imperishable righteousness of God and the dignity of man. History records man's triumphant ascent. Each halt in his progress has been but a pause before a mighty leap forward. The time is not out of joint.

If indeed some of the temples we worshipped in have fallen, we have built new ones on the sacred sites loftier and holier than those which have crumbled. If we have lost some of the heroic physical qualities of our ancestors, we have replaced them with a spiritual nobleness that turns aside wrath and binds up the wounds of the vanquished. All the past attainments of man are ours; and more, his day-dreams have become our clear realities. Therein lies our hope and sure faith.

As I stand in the sunshine of a sincere and earnest optimism, my imagination "paints yet more glorious triumphs on the cloud-curtain of the future." Out of the fierce struggle and turmoil of contending systems and powers I see a brighter spiritual era slowly emerge—an era in which there shall be no England, no France, no Germany, no America, no this people or that, but one family, the human race; one law, peace; one need, harmony; one means, labor; one taskmaster, God.

If I should try to say anew the creed of the optimist, I should say something like this: "I believe in God, I believe in man, I believe in the power of the spirit. I believe it is a sacred duty to encourage ourselves and others; to hold the tongue from any unhappy word against God's world, because no man has any right to complain of a universe which God made good, and which thousands of men have striven to keep good. I believe we should so act that we may draw nearer and more near the age when no man shall live at his ease while another suffers."

These are the articles of my faith, and there is yet another on which all depends—to bear this faith above every tempest which overfloods it, and to make it a principle in disaster and through affliction. Optimism is the harmony between man's spirit and the spirit of God pronouncing His works good.

The End